The Berenstain Bears'
STORYTIME TREASURY

Bibliographical Note

The Berenstain Bears' Storytime Treasury, first published by Dover Publications, Inc., in 2012, is a republication of the following works by Stan and Jan Berenstain: *The Berenstain Bears Are a Family*; *The Berenstain Bears' Four Seasons*; *The Berenstain Bears at the Super-Duper Market*; and *The Berenstain Bears Say Good Night*, all published in 1991 by Random House, Inc.

Library of Congress Cataloging-in-Publication Data

Berenstain, Stan, 1923–2005.
    The Berenstain bears' storytime treasury / Stan and Jan Berenstain.
        v. cm.
    Summary: A collection of four previously published works, three told in rhyme, of the Berenstain bears and their everyday lives.
    Contents: The Berenstain bears are a family — The Berenstain bears' four seasons — The Berenstain bears at the super-duper market — The Berenstain bears say good night.
    ISBN-13: 978-0-486-49836-2
    ISBN-10: 0-486-49836-0
    [1. Stories in rhyme. 2. Bears—Fiction. 3. Families—Fiction. 4. Seasons—Fiction. 5. Supermarkets—Fiction. 6. Bedtime—Fiction.] I. Berenstain, Jan 1923–2012. II. Title.

PZ8.3.B4493Bhjb 2012
[E]—dc23

                                                                2012030159

Manufactured in the United States by LSC Communications
49836007   2020
www.doverpublications.com

Contents

The Berenstain Bears are a FAMILY

Stan & Jan
Berenstain

Mama, Papa,
Sister, Brother,
we're related
to each other.

We four are
a family.
We live together
in this tree.

Yes, we are
a family,
happy in
our Home Sweet Tree.

Family members
help each other.
We help our
father
and our mother.

To be sure,
they help us, too.
There's quite a lot
they help us do.

9

They help us with
our snaps and bows.

They help us wipe
a runny nose.

They help us scrub
behind our ears.

And when we cry,
they dry our tears.

Mother, father,
daughter, son.
We're a family.
We have fun!

We play games,
like tick-tack-toe.

We play ball.
We catch. We throw.

We sing and dance.
We jump. We run.
Mother, daughter,
father, son.
We're a family.
We have fun!

Here come Aunt Dot
and Uncle Ed
and their son,
our cousin Fred.

They're part of
our family, too.
They've come to share
our barbecue.

And don't forget
Gramps and Gran,
the oldest members
of our clan.

We're expecting
them today.
Here they come!
Hooray! Hooray!

We say hooray
for Gramps and Gran.

the oldest members
of our clan!

Even in a family
that usually gets along,
sometimes there are problems,
sometimes things go wrong.

Things get spilled.
Things get broken.

Sometimes unkind
words are spoken.

But we make up.
We work things out.

We don't grumble,
sulk, or pout.

Yes, father, mother,
sister, brother—
we're a *family*.
We understand
and love each other.

The Berenstain Bears'
FOUR SEASONS

Stan & Jan Berenstain

Look out the window.
What do we see?
Green buds growing
on our Home Sweet Tree.

We see crocuses
beginning to show
through what is left
of a Bear Country snow.

That means it's Spring—
when April showers

bring daffodils, tulips,
and other May flowers.

The days get so warm
we know that soon
Summer will come.
It starts in June.

In Summer
it gets very hot.
Mama Bear squirts
the hose a lot.

We help Papa Bear
keep nice and cool.
We let him share
our plastic pool.

Dark thunderclouds
begin to form.
They warn us of
a Summer storm.

Then comes Fall,
which, we remember,
is also called Autumn,
It starts in September.

The colors of Autumn,
red, yellow, and gold,
have been lying in wait
for that first snap of cold.

When the wind blows,
Leaves quiver and shake.
When they fall,
it's time to rake.

"Papa, be careful,"
says Mama Bear.
"Brother and Sister
are under there!"

Another new season,
Winter, is near.
How can we tell
when Winter is here?

Our teeth chatter.

Our knees shiver.

We see ice on the river.

A few snowflakes
begin to fall.

But soon it's a blizzard,
a *big* snowfall.

We go sledding
on Big Bear Hill.
What an adventure!
What a thrill!

Then, one cold
and dreary day,
when it seems that
Winter
has come to stay,
we look outside,
and what do we see?
Spring buds sprouting
on our Home Sweet Tree.

51

Old Earth has circled
around the sun.
Another set of seasons
has begun.

The Berenstain Bears at the SUPER-DUPER MARKET

Stan & Jan Berenstain

We get into our car.
We belt ourselves in.
Our trip to the market
is about to begin.

Some markets are big.
Some markets are super.
Our supermarket
is super-duper.

We park our car.
We get a cart.
Let's go shop.
It's time to start.

The magic doors
open themselves.
Inside are lots of things
On lots of shelves.

What kinds of things
are on the shelves
inside those doors
that open themselves?

What do you suppose?
What do you think?
Everything in the world
to eat and drink.

SALE

FRUITS & VEGETABLES

Milk and honey,

butter and cheese,

potatoes, tomatoes,

cabbage, and peas.

64

Also, such things
as soap and shampoo,
          ballpoint pens,
          toothpaste, and glue.

Paper napkins,
bathroom tissue,
Tree House Keeping—
the latest issue!

And all different kinds
of sweets and toys
to interest little
girls and boys.

CHECK OUT

CANDY
TOYS

Some of us fuss.
Some of us beg.
Some of us grab
our mama's leg.

CHECK OUT

CHECK

CANDY TOYS

Of course, not us,
We never grab
or make a fuss.

And even though
shopping is fun,
we're just as glad
when we are done.

We climb in the car.
We belt ourselves in.
It's time for our
homeward trip to begin.

We've lots of nourishing
food to eat,
and maybe even
a toy or sweet.

And heading home,
as we ride along,
we sing our
supermarket song:

Some markets are big.
Some markets are super.
Our supermarket
is super-duper.

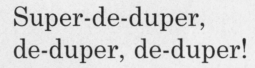

Super-de-duper,
de-duper, de-duper!

The Berenstain Bears
SAY GOOD NIGHT

Stan & Jan
Berenstain

Our friend the sun
is high and bright.
It's not yet time
to say good night.

It still is day,
it seems to say,
there still is time
for us to play.

85

But now the sun
is riding low.
Its light is now
a rosy glow.

Time for our bath.
We get undressed.
Ma helps us start.
We do the rest.

We suds our fur
and rinse our heads.
We're still not ready
for our beds.

Mama dries us.
Ouch! We shout
as Papa combs
our tangles out.

Now we have to
brush our teeth.
The ones on top,
the ones beneath.
We brush and brush
and brush our teeth.

The moon comes out.
We notice that
it's sometimes thin
and sometimes fat.

Is <u>now</u> the time
to say good night?
Our friend the moon
says no, not quite.
It's not yet time
to say good night.

We have to put
our nighties on.
We're getting sleepy.
We stretch. We yawn.

We choose a book.
This one, perhaps.
We climb upon
our parents' laps.

Though others would
do nicely too—
which book you choose
is absolutely
up to you.

Now the time
has come for dozing.
Even Papa's eyes
are closing.

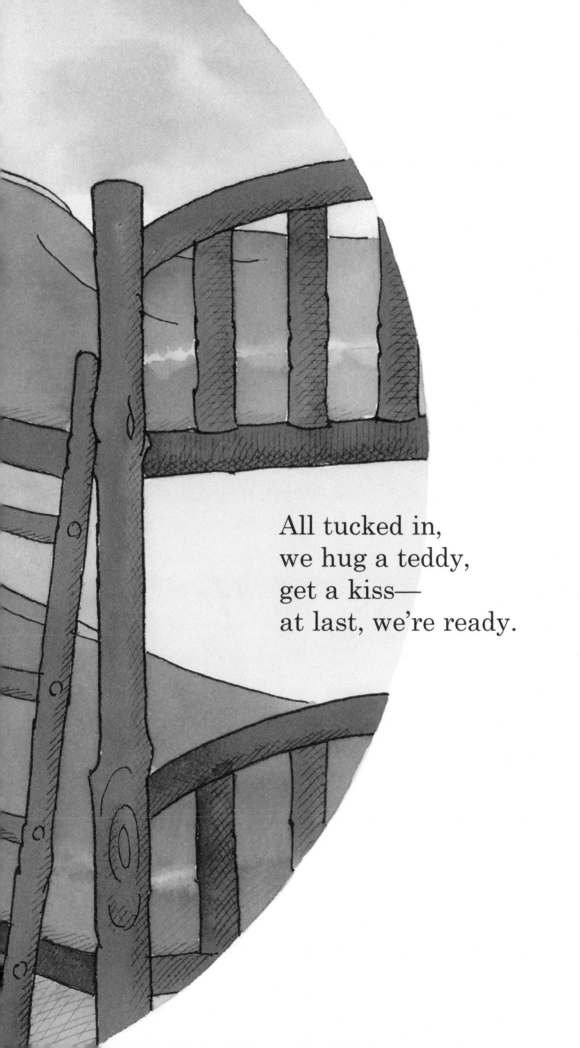

All tucked in,
we hug a teddy,
get a kiss—
at last, we're ready.

With the moon aglow,
the stars so bright,
it's time at last
to say good night.

Good night.
Good night.
Good night.
Good night.

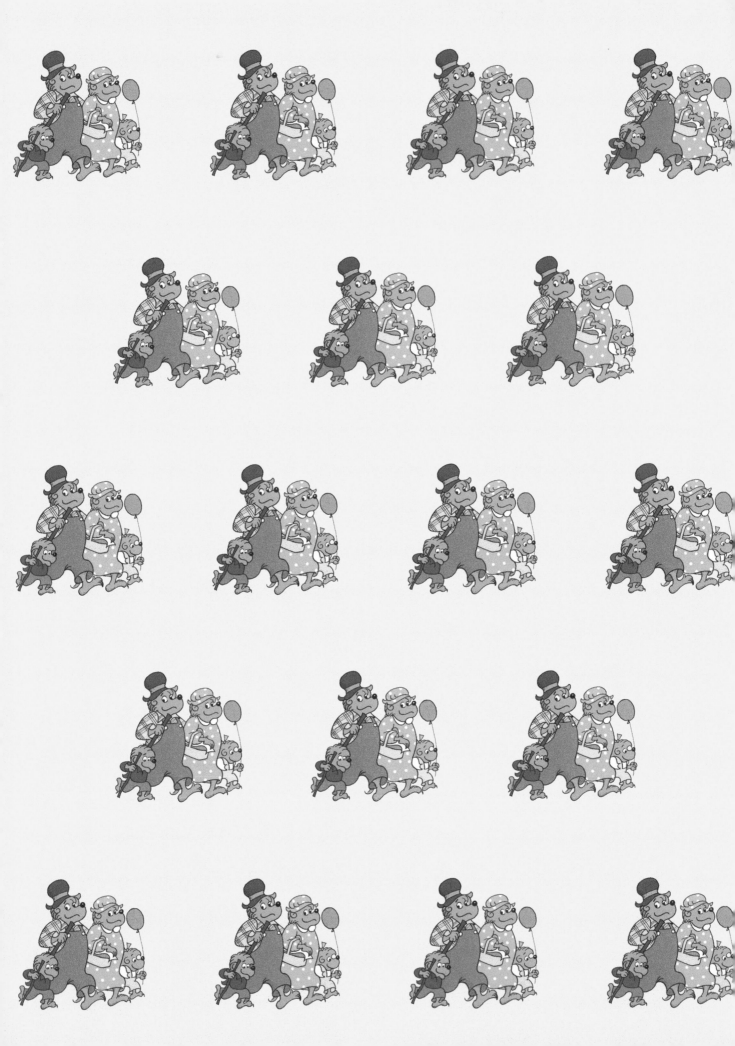